THE MICE NEXT DOOR

Anthony Knowles

Illustrated by Susan Edwards

M

MACMILLAN CHILDREN'S BOOKS

For Oliver and Samuel,
and in memory of my father

Text copyright © 1986 Anthony Knowles
Illustrations copyright © 1986 Susan Edwards

First published 1986 by Hodder & Stoughton Ltd

Picturemac edition published 1988 by
Macmillan Children's Books
A division of Macmillan Publishers Limited
London and Basingstoke
Associated companies throughout the world

Reprinted 1991

British Library Cataloguing in Publication Data
Knowles, Anthony
    The mice next door: and what my Dad
    said about them.——(Picturemac).
    I. Title   II. Edwards, Susan
    823'.914[J]   PZ7
    ISBN 0-333-44977-0

Printed in Hong Kong

It took them only a day to build their house, and when they had finished I went and told Mum and Dad about it. Mum said she really quite liked mice in a funny sort of way, but Dad said I was talking rubbish because mice lived in holes.

Later, while we were having tea, there was a knock on the door. Mum came back followed by four mice. Mum was white-faced. She said: "Mr and Mrs Hardy and their family have come to say 'hello' — they've just moved in next door."

That night I heard Dad say it was outrageous and that it shouldn't be allowed. If God had wanted mice to live in their own houses He wouldn't have made mouse-holes. Dad said he would ring the Council in the morning and have the little pests taken away.

Mum said Dad had been rude to stare at the Hardys.

Dad didn't like the Hardys' house. He said it was not in keeping with the neighbourhood. If something wasn't done about them soon, there would be mice crawling around everywhere. He didn't want mice under the floorboards and he didn't want them living next door. Everyone knew mice were smelly.

Dad said the Hardys were stupid and greedy to order so
much milk, and he told me not to play with Frankie Hardy
because I didn't know where he'd been.

Mum said it was she who had asked the milkman to leave
two bottles for the new neighbours.

Mum told the Hardys to watch out for Biscuit our cat. Mr Hardy looked startled when I told him Biscuit liked mice — but Biscuit played with Frankie and his sister Susan all afternoon.

Dad said enough was enough, and first thing in the morning he'd telephone for a real rat catcher.

A few days later the Hardys had a house-warming party.
Mr Hardy came and told Dad he was sorry not to invite us,
but we were too big.

Dad was speechless.

It was a wonderful party. It went on all night, and
sometimes guests danced on the lawn.

Dad told Mum that we could always expect a lot of noise from the Hardys in the future. Mice were known for the din they made — they were only interested in having a good time.

The day after the party Dad moaned to Mum about the smell of cooking from next door. He said it was an unpleasant nuisance and he was sure the Council would do something about it.

Just before lunch Mrs Hardy came round with a cheese pie for us all. She said it was to make up for us not coming to the party.

One Sunday Mr Hardy took his family out for a ride on his
new motorbike and sidecar.

"Disgraceful," said Dad. "That mouse is lowering the tone of the village. He should have a car like ordinary folk."

Mum said: "We had a motorbike when we first got married."

About a month after they moved in the Hardys built a shed and erected a fence around their garden. Dad said they probably did not have planning permission, and he wasn't going to stand for it.

Mr and Mrs Hardy kept their garden very neat and tidy. They were always weeding, and cutting the grass and planting flowers.

Dad said it was most unusual for mice to care about their gardens.

One day Little Frankie stuck his tongue out at Dad while Dad was tidying up our garden.

"The trouble with mice," said Dad later, "is that they just don't have decent manners. The parents never teach their youngsters how to behave." In the evening Mr Hardy brought Frankie round to apologise.

Next morning Dad caught Frankie eating nuts on our
bird-table. Dad was furious and called him a wretched little
thief. Frankie was frightened and chattered his teeth. He
cried and said they were his nuts that I had taken from him,
and I told Dad that what Frankie said was true.

Dad and I both went to bed early that night.

Quite often Mrs Hardy, Frankie and Susan would have a
cup of tea with us when Dad was out at work.

When Dad found out about this he didn't say anything, but he made a big show of looking under the kitchen floorboards with a torch.

The day Mr Hardy painted his front door Dad said it was time to sell our house and move to a more respectable neighbourhood.

Mum said she rather liked to see a bit of colour, and no one was ever going to make her leave her home — even though it was tatty and needed repainting.

For several weeks Dad refused to have anything to do with the Hardys. But one day in the late autumn, when our drain-pipe got blocked with leaves and Dad couldn't budge them, Mr Hardy poked his head through the fence and asked if there was anything he could do to help.

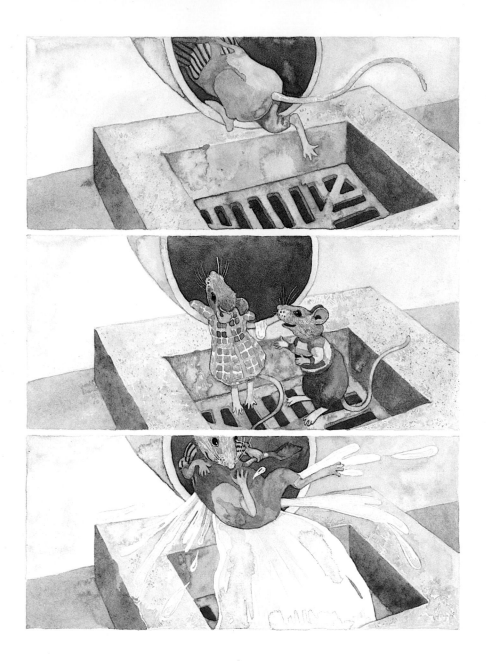

Dad said he doubted that a rodent could do what a man couldn't, but when Mr Hardy managed the job in a way that only he could, Dad was very grateful.

In fact, by the time he'd finished, Mr Hardy had us all laughing — including Dad.

During that night it snowed heavily and unexpectedly. As soon as Dad saw the snow and what was visible of the Hardys' house he rushed round next door with a shovel.

"I was just repaying a favour," said Dad when we were having breakfast. "I'd have done it for anyone."

After breakfast Mum, Dad and I went into the garden to build a snowman. Suddenly a little snowball hit Dad on the back of his head.

Dad wasn't at all cross with Frankie, in fact Dad threw a little snowball back at him — and then before we knew it we and the Hardys were all having a snowball fight.

Mum and Dad decided to have a big bonfire party on
November 5th, and all our friends and neighbours were to
be invited. Sadly, Frankie and Susie went down with
measles on the day, and had to stay in bed.

Dad suggested that we should have the party at the side of
the house so Frankie and Susie would be able to see.

The following Saturday afternoon Dad was disturbed from
his nap by a light tapping on the front door. It was Frankie.
He was better and he wanted to know if Dad and I could
come out to play.

We played football until it was dark, and then Dad invited all the Hardys round for tea.

Mum was pleased, but she said she wished she had known earlier that they were coming.

On Sunday night when I was in bed, Mr Hardy brought round three dozen bottles of his home-brewed cheese wine that he'd mentioned to Dad the evening before.

Mr Hardy drank three bottles and Dad finished the rest.

They fell asleep in our living room, and were both late for
work on Monday morning.

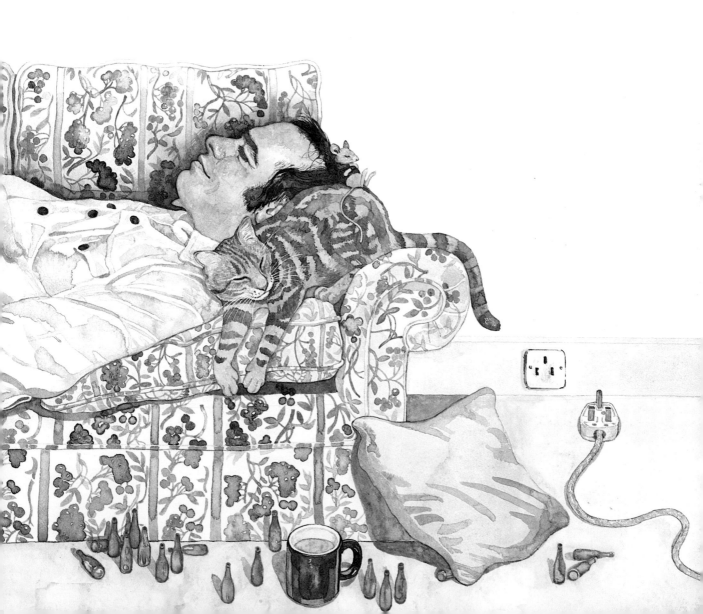

The following Sunday Dad asked the Hardys round for lunch.